blah blah blah blah blah blah blah blah blah blah blah blah blah blah blah blah blah blah blah blah blah blah blah blah

Raintree is an imprint of Capstone Global Library Limited,
a company incorporated in England and Wales having its
registered office at 7 Pilgrim Street, London, EC4V 6LB –
Registered company number: 6695582

To contact Raintree:
Phone: 0845 6044371
Fax: + 44 (0) 1865 312263
Email: myorders@raintreepublishers.co.uk
Outside the UK please telephone +44 1865 312262.

First published by © Picture Window Books in 2011
First published in the United Kingdom in paperback in 2014
The moral rights of the proprietor have been asserted.

Designer: Kay Fraser
Editor: Catherine Veitch
Originated by Capstone Global LIbrary Ltd

ISBN 978 1 47476 572 5 (paperback)
21 20 19 18 17
10 9 8 7 6 5 4 3 2 1

British Library Cataloguing in Publication Data
A full catalogue record for this book is available from the British Library.

Printed and bound in India

BELLA
the Storyteller

written by Adam and Charlotte Guillain.
illustrated by Richard Watson

Bella **loved** to tell stories to her friends.

She loved stories **SO** much...

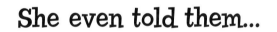

She even told them...

...to herself!

Bella told stories at lunchtime.

She told stories at school - even in **maths!**

Bella told stories to her brother when he was trying to watch TV.

She even told stories to her dad when she should have been cleaning her teeth.

Nothing could stop Bella telling stories.

But one day Bella woke up and found that she had **lost her voice.**

She tried to whisper.

She tried to **SHOUT!**

Bella tried to **sing**.

But no words came out.

Poor Bella! She couldn't tell stories at breakfast.

But she did listen to her family as they happily **chatted away.**

She even had time to finish **all her homework** before school!

Bella couldn't tell stories on her way to
school that day, so she listened to her
friend Becky telling jokes instead.

"Becky's jokes are **hilarious**," thought Bella. "When I get my voice back I must ask her to tell me a few more."

Bella couldn't tell stories at school.

But she got a **gold star** for finishing all her maths work in double-quick time.

"She'll probably get another gold star for **great** listening," thought her teacher.

After school, Bella still couldn't tell stories,
so she watched TV with her brother.

"This monster cartoon is really **great**," she thought.

At bedtime, Bella brushed her teeth, put on her pyjamas, and got into bed, ready for her dad to read to her.

They even had time to read **two extra stories!**

The next morning, Bella woke up feeling **fine**.

"**Hurray!**" she cried. "I can start telling stories again."

Bella bounded down the stairs, **talking** all the way.

"Oh my goodness! I have so much
to say," she told Mum. "Becky is so funny. I got a
gold star for my maths. I saw a great cartoon and..."

Bella **stopped** talking. She remembered why she had all these great stories and decided to eat her breakfast.

Her family talked and talked and talked
while Bella happily **listened**.

Bella still **loves** to tell stories.

But now she likes to **listen** to them, too.